Miranda
the Beauty
Fairy

Special thanks to Narinder Dhami

ISBN 978-0-545-48483-1

12 11 10 9 8 7 6 5 4 3 2 1   13 14 15 16 17 18/0

Printed in the U.S.A.   40

This edition first printing, July 2013

Miranda the Beauty Fairy

by Daisy Meadows

SCHOLASTIC INC.

The Fairyland Palace

Tippington Fountains SHOPPING CENTER

Top Hats & Tiaras

FASHION

HARTLEYS

↑ Ice Blue Hair Salon

Fashion Show

TIPPINGTON TOYS

Ice Blue booth ←

I'm the king of designer fashion,
Looking stylish is my passion.
Ice Blue's the name of my fashion line,
The designs are fabulous and they're all mine!

Some people think my clothes are odd,
But I will get the fashion world's nod.
Fashion Fairy magic will make my dream come true —
Soon everyone will wear Ice Blue!

Contents

A Splash of Magic

"This is amazing, Rachel!" Kirsty exclaimed. Her eyes wide, she stared up at the enormous glittering steel-and-glass building in front of them. Across the entrance was a sign that said TIPPINGTON FOUNTAINS SHOPPING CENTER in blue lights.

"Yes, isn't it?" Rachel agreed. "I'm so glad you're staying with me for the

1

break so you could be here for the grand opening, Kirsty."

"Me, too," Kirsty said eagerly. "And I'm really looking forward to seeing Jessica Jarvis!" The famous supermodel was the special guest at the new shopping mall's opening ceremony. A crowd of people had already gathered, waiting for the ceremony to begin.

"I think we're just in time for the parade," Mrs. Walker said, locking her car. "Come on, girls."

Rachel, Kirsty, and Mrs. Walker hurried to join the crowd. Moments later, the first float appeared around the side of the building.

"Every shop in the mall has its own float, Kirsty," Rachel explained. "Look, the first one is Tippington Toys."

The float rumbled slowly toward them. A huge inflatable teddy bear sat on the back of the truck. Also on the float were two girls dressed as rag dolls with ruffled dresses and pigtails made of yellow yarn, as well as a boy wearing a red soldier uniform. They waved to the crowd as they passed by.

"The next one is the Book Nook," Kirsty said, reading the painted banner draped across the float.

The Book Nook's float carried people dressed as characters from storybooks. The girls spotted Snow White, Cinderella, Pinocchio, and several others. The Sweet Scoop Ice Cream Parlor float came next, with its giant foam ice-cream cones and ice pops.

"That ice cream looks yummy!" Kirsty laughed.

Rachel sniffed the air. "I can smell something yummy, too," she said. "So can I," Kirsty replied as delicious smells wafted past her nose. "Strawberries and vanilla!"

"The Bath Bliss float is coming," Mrs. Walker said. "They sell hair and body products."

A banner that stretched across the float declared, WE ONLY USE NATURAL ORGANIC INGREDIENTS! Rachel and Kirsty laughed when they saw that the float carried bubble machines that were spraying hundreds of shimmering, scented bubbles into the crowd.

"Magical!" Rachel sighed. She caught a strawberry-scented bubble on her finger. "They look like fairy bubbles, Kirsty!"

The girls exchanged a quick smile. Their

friendship with the fairies was a *very* special secret.

"Look, girls, here's the last float," Mrs. Walker said a little while later. "Can you see who's on it?"

"Jessica Jarvis!" Rachel and Kirsty announced excitedly.

Jessica sat on a plush golden throne, waving to the crowd. She wore a sapphire-colored dress, and her long

blond hair was twisted elegantly on top of her head. "She's so pretty," Kirsty murmured. Everyone cheered as the float stopped outside the doors

of the shopping mall. A small platform
with a microphone had been set up, and
a group of local politicians,
including the mayor,
in her official robes,
were waiting. Rachel
and Kirsty could see
a red ribbon tied
across the doors.

Jessica Jarvis
stepped down from
the float and onto the
stage to thunderous applause.

"Good morning, everyone," Jessica
said, smiling. "I'm so happy to be here
to open this wonderful new shopping
mall, Tippington Fountains. But before I
do, I have a very special announcement
to make. . . ."

Rachel and Kirsty listened eagerly.

"The owners of the shopping center have asked me to announce a brand-new children's competition," Jessica went on. "We want you to design and make your own outfits! They'll be judged two days from now, and the winners will model them in a charity fashion show at the end of this week."

There was more applause.

"And the design competition isn't about looking like a model," Jessica added. "It's all about using your imagination and coming up with a unique outfit."

"Should we enter, Kirsty?" Rachel said.

"Definitely!" Kirsty agreed.

The mayor handed Jessica a large pair of scissors.

"And now . . ." Jessica said, "I know you're eager to see all the fabulous new stores. So I declare this shopping mall open!" With a flourish, she cut the red ribbon in half.

There was more applause as the glass doors swung open. Then the girls and Mrs. Walker followed the rest of the crowd into the mall.

"It's just as beautiful inside as outside!" Kirsty declared, staring around in awe.

Disco-ball lights and enormous hanging baskets holding lush green ferns dangled from the tall glass ceilings, and the floors were decorated with swirling patterns of silver mosaic tiles. Kirsty could hardly believe how many different stores there were, all with wonderful window displays.

"The fountains in the middle of the
mall are supposed to be spectacular, too,"
said Mrs. Walker.

"Oh, can we see them?" Rachel asked.

"You and Kirsty
go ahead, and I'll
meet you back here
in half an hour,"
Mrs. Walker
suggested. "One of
the stores is offering
free makeovers."
She pointed to a
nearby beauty-supply store, Beautiful
You. "I thought I'd try a new look for
the party we're going to this weekend."

Rachel grinned. "Great idea, Mom.
You can surprise Dad!"

Mrs. Walker laughed. "See you later, girls," she said.

The girls were walking through the shopping mall when Kirsty suddenly gave Rachel a nudge.

"Look!" Kirsty whispered. "It's Jessica Jarvis!"

Jessica was standing next to the press booth. A woman was interviewing her while a photographer snapped pictures.

"They're probably from the local paper," Rachel guessed. "Oh, look, Kirsty — the fountains!"

The girls had reached the center of the mall and, as Mrs. Walker had said, the fountains were spectacular. The central fountain was in the middle of a large, clear blue pool. It shot a sparkling jet of water almost as high as the mall ceiling. Around the big fountain was a circle of smaller fountains that sprayed water every so often. There was a cascading

waterfall at one end of the pool, and the whole area was surrounded by huge pots of tropical flowers in vivid shades of red and orange.

"It's gorgeous!" Kirsty exclaimed as she and Rachel paused by the edge of the pool.

Suddenly, the small fountain closest to them sprayed a burst of water. The girls jumped in surprise as they felt a few drops splash their faces.

Then Kirsty glanced up and noticed a tiny, bright sparkle on top of the fountain.

"Rachel," she whispered, pointing upward. "Look! What's that?"

"I'm not sure," Rachel whispered back. "Could it be . . . a fairy?"

The Fashion
Fairies

As Rachel and Kirsty watched, the
sparkle swirled down from the top of
the fountain. It floated toward one of the
pots and landed on a trumpet-shaped
scarlet flower. Now the excited girls
could see that the sparkle really *was* a
tiny fairy.

"Kirsty, it's Phoebe the Fashion Fairy!"

Rachel gasped as she recognized their old friend.

Phoebe stood on tiptoe on one of the flower petals, waving her wand. "Hello,

girls," she called in her sweet voice. "It's wonderful to see you again."

"Hello, Phoebe!" Kirsty smiled at her. "How are you, and how are all the other Party Fairies?"

"Everyone in Fairyland is fine, and they're all hoping to see you very soon," Phoebe replied, her eyes twinkling. "That's why I'm here, to invite you to come back to Fairyland with me!"

Rachel and Kirsty were thrilled.

"A big fashion show is taking place in the grand hall of the Fairyland Palace," Phoebe explained. "It's been organized by my seven helpers, the Fashion Fairies. Would you like to come?"

"Yes, please!" Kirsty and Rachel said together, sounding so eager that Phoebe laughed. She flitted out of sight behind the fountain, and the girls rushed to join her. With one wave of Phoebe's wand, a cloud of glittering fairy magic surrounded Rachel and Kirsty. It turned them into fairies and gently carried them away to Fairyland.

Just a few seconds later, Phoebe, Rachel, and Kirsty arrived in the grand hall of the royal palace. King Oberon and Queen Titania were seated on their golden  thrones, and the other fairies were sitting around a long catwalk, waiting for the fashion show to begin.

"Phoebe brought Kirsty and Rachel!" called Amber the Orange Fairy, and there were whoops of delight.

"Welcome, girls!" said Pearl the Cloud Fairy.

"We're so glad you could join us," India the Moonstone Fairy added.

Phoebe escorted a smiling Rachel and Kirsty over to the king and queen.

"Girls, we're thrilled to have you with us again!" King Oberon declared.

"The Fashion Fairies always put on a fabulous show," Queen Titania told them. "Phoebe, why don't you introduce Rachel and Kirsty to your helpers?"

Phoebe nodded. She led the girls over to the front row of the audience, where seven fairies were seated.

"Girls, meet Miranda the Beauty Fairy, Claudia the Accessories Fairy, Tyra the Designer Fairy, Alexa the Fashion Reporter Fairy, Jennifer the Hairstylist Fairy, Brooke the Photographer Fairy, and Lola the Fashion Show Fairy," Phoebe said, pointing her wand at each fairy in turn.

"Hello, girls!" the Fashion Fairies called. Rachel and Kirsty could see that each fairy had an object that shimmered with magic. Miranda held a golden tube of lipstick, Claudia wore a long necklace with many charms, Tyra had a tape measure, Alexa had a pen, Jennifer had a hairbrush, and Brooke carried a camera. The seventh fairy, Lola, had a special backstage pass with a ribbon that went around her neck.

"With the help of our magical objects, we look after all kinds of fashion in both the human and the fairy worlds," Miranda the Beauty Fairy explained. She had light brown hair and wore cropped jeans, a pink top, and a blue jacket with a furry collar.

Suddenly, there was a fanfare of trumpets. Bertram the frog footman stepped out from behind the magnificent velvet curtains.

"It's time for the fashion
show to begin!" he
announced with a bow.

Rachel and Kirsty
hurried to take their
places next to the king
and queen. Meanwhile,
Phoebe stepped up
onto the catwalk.

"Our very first model is Ruby the Red
Fairy," Phoebe announced. Rachel and
Kirsty clapped loudly. Ruby was their
oldest friend, the very first fairy they'd
met on their trip to Rainspell Island.

There was a round of applause as
Ruby stepped out from behind the
curtains. She looked beautiful in a red
silk dress with a full skirt that swirled
around her ankles.

Rachel and Kirsty watched as Ruby walked to the end of the catwalk and twirled. But at that moment, a freezing ice bolt zoomed from the back of the hall and crackled over their heads. The girls covered their mouths in horror as the ice bolt crashed onto the catwalk. Ruby gave a little scream. Then, to everyone's amazement, Ruby's dress turned from red to a pale icy-blue color.

"What's happening?" Rachel gasped. "Ruby's dress changed color, and look! A picture appeared on her skirt!"

Kirsty stared at the picture. "I don't believe it!" she said shakily. "Rachel, it's a picture of Jack Frost!"

Ice Blue

Rachel, Kirsty, and the fairies watched, shocked, as Ruby stared down at her dress in disbelief. Suddenly, Jack Frost appeared at the back of the hall, riding on an ice bolt. He hurtled toward the catwalk, a smug grin on his frosty face. He was followed by a gaggle of goblins.

"What's Jack Frost up to now?" Kirsty whispered to Rachel as he jumped off the ice bolt and onto the catwalk.

"And what's he *wearing*?" Rachel murmured, hardly able to believe her eyes.

Jack Frost was dressed in an ice-blue jacket with enormous shoulder pads. He wore clunky, unlaced boots and tight leggings with a star pattern. The goblins were also wearing strange, mismatched outfits. One wore a top hat and a pair of blue shorts, while another sported a blue jacket with a bow tie and a blue T-shirt.

"Clear the catwalk!" Jack Frost shouted, glaring at Ruby and Phoebe. "The style king is here!"

The goblins applauded as Jack Frost paraded up and down the catwalk.

"Our outfits are from a stylish new fashion label called Ice Blue," Jack Frost declared. "And guess what? All the clothes are designed by ME!"

"But you're not a fashion designer, Jack Frost!" Tyra the Designer Fairy said in horror.

Jack Frost shot her an icy glare. "We'll see about that!" he declared. "I know all about fashion, and I'm so handsome, I want everyone to look like me." He strutted along the catwalk, pausing every few steps to make an awkward pose. "Soon every single human and all the fairies will ONLY wear clothes by Ice Blue. Just think how stylish everyone will be!"

Rachel and Kirsty glanced at each other in dismay as the goblins went wild. Then Queen Titania stood up.

"This is all very silly, Jack Frost," the queen said sternly. "But you're welcome to stay and watch our fashion show if you'll turn Ruby's dress red again."

"I don't think so!" Jack Frost sneered. Raising his wand, he sent an ice bolt flying straight toward Queen Titania. Bertram sprang up to defend her, but he couldn't stop Jack Frost's spell. The queen's golden crown vanished and was replaced by a blue wool hat with a huge pom-pom on top.

"How dare you, Jack Frost!" scolded King Oberon, looking very upset. He jumped to his feet as Bertram helped the queen remove the silly hat. "You've gone too far this time."

"And I'm not finished yet!" Jack Frost cackled. He pointed his ice wand at the seven Fashion Fairies in the front row. Instantly, a flurry of ice bolts zoomed toward them. Rachel and Kirsty watched helplessly as Jack Frost's magic swept all of the Fashion Fairies' magical objects away, even lifting Claudia's necklace and Lola's backstage pass over their heads.

The goblins roared with laughter as the objects flew across the catwalk and into Jack Frost's enormous pockets.

"Now that I have all the Fashion Fairies' magic, I'm off to Tippington to win the charity fashion show!" Jack Frost announced. "Then soon everyone, everywhere will be wearing my beautiful Ice Blue clothes!"

"Wait!" King Oberon shouted.

But Jack Frost waved his wand. Then he and his goblins disappeared in an icy-blue mist.

"This is terrible!" Miranda the Beauty Fairy said. "Our fashion show is ruined!"

"Nothing will go right now," Lola the Fashion Show Fairy agreed, biting her lip.

"That means the charity fashion show in the human world will be a disaster, too," Claudia the Accessories Fairy pointed out. "In fact, fashion everywhere will be ruined unless we get our magical objects back!"

"Rachel and I can help!" Kirsty said, her eyes shining with determination.

"We'll do our best to find *all* the magical objects," Rachel promised.

"Girls, you are coming to our rescue once again," Queen Titania said gratefully. "Thank you for being such loyal friends."

"Miranda the Beauty Fairy will return to Tippington Fountains with you," King Oberon told Rachel and Kirsty. "Good luck with your search."

"Good luck!" the fairies all cried. Miranda waved her wand, and the girls returned to their human size. With another flick of Miranda's wand, the three vanished in a cloud of fairy magic.

Makeover Mayhem

"It's almost time to meet my mom at Beautiful You," Rachel said as they arrived back at the fountains. "We can look for Miranda's magic lipstick on the way."

Miranda nodded and hid inside Kirsty's denim purse.

Quickly, the girls retraced their steps

through the mall. There were lots of
people around, and Rachel wondered
how they would spot the missing lipstick
in the enormous crowd. But then she
remembered what Queen Titania always
said: *"Let the magic come to you."*

The Beautiful You shop was very
busy. Through the windows, Rachel and
Kirsty could see lots of women sitting on
stools at the makeup counters, getting
makeovers.

"There's my mom," Rachel said, spotting
the back of her
mother's head. A girl
in a short-sleeved white
smock was applying
blush to Mrs. Walker's
cheeks with a large,
fluffy brush.

Rachel and Kirsty went into the shop, and Miranda stayed out of sight. Beautiful You was filled with shelves of all kinds of makeup in every color imaginable. The girls looked closely at the different lipsticks as they passed by, but none of them shimmered with fairy magic.

"Hi, Mom," said Rachel, tapping Mrs. Walker on the shoulder.

Rachel's mom turned around, and the girls gasped in shock. Mrs. Walker's face was caked in heavy makeup. Her eye shadow was emerald green, her mascara was bright blue, and she had two circles of deep red blush, one on each cheek. She looked like a circus clown!

"What's the matter?" Mrs. Walker asked, turning around to look in the mirror. She stared at herself in complete horror. "Oh, my goodness! I look awful!"

"I'm *so* sorry," the girl in the white smock mumbled. She seemed embarrassed.  "I don't know what's wrong with me today."

The girls glanced around the room. Rachel's mom wasn't the only woman getting a terrible makeover. There were plenty of other customers who looked disappointed. Their faces were all caked in thick and unflattering makeup.

"This is all because my magical lipstick is missing!" Miranda whispered from Kirsty's bag. "All the makeup looks horrible, and everyone has lost the smile that makes them naturally beautiful."

"Maybe we can help you fix it, Mom," Rachel suggested, but Mrs. Walker shook her head gloomily.

"I'm going to the ladies' room to wipe it all off," she said, sliding off her stool. "Why don't you girls meet me at the Sweet Scoop Ice Cream Parlor in twenty minutes?"

"OK, Mom," Rachel replied.

"Maybe we should take a closer look around this store before we go," Kirsty whispered to Rachel as Mrs. Walker left. "It's the perfect place to hide the magic lipstick! No one would notice it here."

Rachel and Kirsty began to wander quietly around Beautiful You, keeping their eyes open for Miranda's magical object. A few minutes later, Rachel noticed three women sitting in a corner. They all had long, flowing hair, and they were doing makeovers on one another, applying lipstick and patting on face powder. Rachel could tell that two of the women looked just as badly made-up as her mom and the other customers. But she was surprised to see that the third woman didn't look the same at all! *Her*

makeup was simple and beautiful, and she was smiling happily.

"Isn't that weird, Kirsty?" Rachel murmured, pointing out the woman to her friend. "Why does *her* makeup look so good?"

Kirsty was about to reply when she noticed the clothes the three women were wearing. All of them were dressed in ice-blue outfits exactly the same color as Jack Frost's jacket.

"Rachel, they're goblins!" Kirsty whispered. "Look at their clothes! They must be wearing wigs, and the face powder is hiding their green skin."

"And the one who is smiling and has such perfect makeup must also have my lipstick!" Miranda realized. "Jack Frost must have given it to the goblins to hide."

"And now they're distracted, playing around with all this makeup!" Rachel guessed. "So how are we going to get the lipstick back?"

Pond Scum
Perfume!

Before the girls and Miranda could
decide on a plan, the three goblins got
up and left the store.

"I'll turn you into fairies," Miranda
decided. "That will make it much easier
to follow the goblins. Otherwise, we
might lose them in the crowd."

Rachel and Kirsty quickly ducked

behind the nearest makeup counter. With just one flick of Miranda's wand, the girls began to shrink. They became smaller and smaller until they were fairy-size, with fluttery wings like Miranda's on their shoulders.

Miranda motioned to the girls. They silently flew from behind the makeup counter and out of the store. At once, they spotted the goblins staring into the window of a chocolate shop, pressing their noses against the glass. Miranda and the girls flew toward them. They kept out of sight by flitting behind the pillars and banners. But then the goblins were on the move again.

"Have you noticed all the shoppers look just as miserable as the people in Beautiful You?" Kirsty asked, frowning. "We *have to* get Miranda's lipstick back — and all the other magical objects, too!"

The goblins had now reached the fountains in the middle of the mall. They squealed with delight and stopped to admire their reflections in the clear blue pool.

"This could be our chance!" Miranda decided.

Kirsty sniffed the air. "What is that horrible smell?" she asked, wrinkling her nose and making a face.

"It smells like pond scum!" Rachel said. "Where's it coming from?"

Miranda pointed at the Bath Bliss shop on the other side of the pool. "All of Bath Bliss's products smell awful because my lipstick is missing!" she explained.

Kirsty could see that the shoppers walking past Bath Bliss were holding their noses in disgust. "The goblins don't seem to mind," she remarked, gazing down at them. They were still staring at their reflections in the water.

"Oh, goblins love bad smells!" Miranda told her.

Just then, Rachel spotted a big sign in the Bath Bliss window.

"Try our beautiful bubbles for free!" she read aloud. *"We're giving away a free trial bottle of our chocolate-and-orange-scented bubble bath, while supplies last."* There was a big stack of bubble-bath bottles next to the sign.

Rachel's face lit up. "Oh, that gave me an idea!" she exclaimed. "But I need to be my normal size again, Miranda."

The three friends flew to hide behind another pillar, and Miranda's magic quickly turned Rachel to her human size again. Immediately, Rachel hurried to Bath Bliss, while Kirsty and Miranda fluttered over to the pot of tropical flowers closest to the three goblins. There, they hid inside one of the large scarlet blooms.

The horrible smell grew even stronger
as Rachel went inside Bath Bliss, so
she wasn't surprised that the shop was

empty. The
girl sitting
behind the
counter looked
miserable.
"Hello, can
I help you?"
she said.
"Could I try one
of your free bottles of bubble bath?"
Rachel asked, pointing at the window
display.

"Are you sure?" the girl asked with a
sigh. "I don't know what happened with
this batch, but something went wrong.
They smell really bad!"

"I'd really like one," Rachel assured her. The shop assistant took a bottle out of the window and handed it to her. Rachel thanked her and then hurried back to the fountains. To her relief, the three goblins were still there.

"Oh, hello!" Rachel said. "I just had to come over and tell you that I think you all look very beautiful."

The goblins smiled smugly.

"We already know that!" said the one with perfect makeup.

"Maybe one day *you'll* be as beautiful as we are, if you try hard enough!" one of the others told Rachel. All three goblins roared with laughter. Meanwhile, Kirsty and Miranda were peeking out of the tropical flower, watching what was going on.

"Wouldn't you like to *smell* beautiful, too?" Rachel asked, holding out the bottle of bubble bath. "Maybe the three of you would like to share this."

The third goblin grabbed the bubble bath, twisted off the cap, and smelled it. "Ooh, yum!" He sighed. "I'm keeping it all for myself."

"I'm the most beautiful, so I should get it!" the goblin with the perfect makeup insisted. He grabbed for the bottle, but the other goblin held it high above his head, out of his reach. Rachel smiled as the third goblin snuck up behind the second goblin, jumped up high, and snatched the bottle. Laughing triumphantly, he waved it in the air.

"Give me that!" shouted the goblin with the perfect makeup. He lunged

at the bottle, and all three goblins began wrestling for it. As they did, the top of the bottle flew off.

Rachel waited quietly as Miranda and Kirsty flew out of the scarlet flower. They circled the goblins, trying to spot the lipstick. Kirsty managed to slip her hand into the pocket of the goblin with the good makeup. To her dismay, it was empty, and she didn't have time to search his other pocket. Quickly, she and Miranda flew behind

one of the pots of flowers again before
the goblins saw them.

There was a sudden splash as the bottle
slipped through the goblins' fingers and
fell into the pool.

"Now look what you've done, you
fool!" the goblins all shouted at one
another.

The water began frothing up into big
soapy bubbles. Rachel made a face as the
smell of pond scum grew stronger, too.

"Oh, that smell's getting worse!" a
passing shopper said to her friend.

"Such pretty perfume!" One of the
goblins sighed happily, as he flicked
some of the bubbles at the others.

That was when an idea popped into
Kirsty's head!

Miranda's Magic Bubbles

"Miranda, could you use your magic to make *a lot* more of the stinky bubbles? We need to distract the goblins," Kirsty whispered.

"Of course!" Miranda said, surprised. She pointed her wand at the fountain pool, and a few magical sparkles landed on the surface of the water. The water began to foam and froth. Hundreds of bubbles appeared and floated up into the air, drifting around the goblins. The smell of pond scum was now so overpowering that the shoppers who were nearby ran for cover. Rachel covered her nose with both hands.

"Bubbles!" shrieked the goblins with delight. "Beautiful, smelly bubbles!" They began scooping up armfuls of bubbles and throwing them at one another.

Kirsty motioned to Miranda. They both took a deep breath, held their noses, and flew out from behind the pot of flowers. They watched the goblins for any sign of Miranda's magical lipstick.

The goblins were running around the fountain, enjoying their bubble fight and getting very wet. Suddenly, Kirsty saw

something golden
fall to the ground
and roll across the
floor of the mall.
It was the magic
lipstick! But the
goblins were having
so much fun, they
didn't even notice.

Kirsty and Miranda flew toward it as
fast as they could. As soon as Miranda
touched the lipstick, it immediately shrank
down to its Fairyland size. Miranda
picked it up, smiling at Kirsty, and
Rachel clapped her hands with delight.

In an instant, the stink of pond scum
vanished and was replaced with the
yummy, rich scent of chocolate and
oranges.

"Yuck!" one of the goblins shouted, making a face. Rachel noticed that his beautiful makeup had started to disappear. "What's that *horrible* smell?"

"Let's get out of here!" another yelled. Holding their noses, they scurried out of the mall.

The shoppers began to return, and Rachel hurried to join Kirsty and Miranda, who were hiding behind one of the small fountains.

"Look, everyone's smiling again, and there are lots of customers going into the Bath Bliss store!" Rachel pointed out.

"And everyone's crazy makeup is much more natural now," Kirsty added as she saw some of the customers from Beautiful You walking by.

"I'm smiling, too!" Miranda said with a big grin. "Thank you so much, girls. You did it again! Everyone in Fairyland will be thrilled when I return with *this*!" She held up her lipstick. "But you will keep looking for the other magical objects, won't you?"

"We promise!" the girls said.

Quickly, Miranda's magic turned Kirsty

back to her human size. Then, waving her wand in farewell, Miranda disappeared in a puff of rainbow-colored magic.

"Time to meet my mom at the Sweet Scoop Ice Cream Parlor," Rachel said, glancing up at a clock.

"I think we deserve a little celebration!" Kirsty laughed.

The girls hurried off.

"You know, I've been thinking about the design competition," Kirsty remarked as they waited outside the ice-cream parlor for Mrs. Walker. "All those bright, tropical flowers around the fountain gave me some ideas!"

"I'd like to use lots of colors in my outfit, too," Rachel agreed. "Oh, here comes Mom — and she looks like herself again, thank goodness!"

Mrs. Walker was coming toward them, smiling. To the girls' relief, her clown makeup had vanished, and she looked naturally beautiful again.

"Everyone's happy now that Miranda's lipstick is back where it belongs," said Kirsty.

"But there are still six magical objects missing," Rachel reminded her. "I hope we find the next one very soon!"

Kirsty and Rachel helped Miranda
find her magic lipstick.
Now it's time for them to help

Claudia
the Accessories Fairy!

Read on for a special sneak peek. . . .

A Hole Lot of Trouble

"Here we are," Mr. Walker said, parking the car at Tippington Fountains Shopping Center. He glanced over to where his daughter, Rachel, and her best friend, Kirsty Tate, were sitting in the backseat. "I know you girls were here yesterday, but I need to pick up a shirt. I'll be as quick as I can."

"Don't worry, Dad," Rachel said, exchanging a secret smile with Kirsty as they got out of the car. "We don't mind at all. Take as long as you need!"

It was the second day of school vacation, and Kirsty was staying with Rachel's family. Whenever the two friends got together, magical things always seemed to happen — and they certainly had yesterday! Rachel's mom had taken the girls to the new mall to be part of the opening-day celebration. There were lots of free activities and a whole parade with colorful floats. It had been really fun and exciting . . . especially when the girls found themselves whisked off to Fairyland and thrown into an exciting brand-new fairy adventure. Hooray!

"I hope we meet another fairy today," Kirsty whispered eagerly to Rachel, as they made their way through the parking lot to the elevators.

"Oh, me too," Rachel replied. "Yesterday was amazing. But you know what Queen Titania always says: We can't go looking for magic. We have to wait for it to come to us." She grinned. "I just hope it finds us again soon!"

The three of them went up in the elevator. "First floor," a voice from the speaker announced after a few moments. "Welcome to Tippington Fountains Shopping Center!"

RAINBOW magic™

There's Magic in Every Series!

The Rainbow Fairies
The Weather Fairies
The Jewel Fairies
The Pet Fairies
The Fun Day Fairies
The Petal Fairies
The Dance Fairies
The Music Fairies
The Sports Fairies
The Party Fairies
The Ocean Fairies
The Night Fairies
The Magical Animal Fairies
The Princess Fairies
The Superstar Fairies

Read them all!

SCHOLASTIC

scholastic.com
rainbowmagiconline.com

HiT entertainment

RMFAIRY7

RAINBOW magic

These activities are magical!
Play dress-up, send friendship notes, and much more!

www.scholastic.com
www.rainbowmagiconline.com

HiT entertainment

RMACTIV3

RAINBOW magic™

SPECIAL EDITION

Three Books in Each One—
More Rainbow Magic Fun!

Joy the Summer Vacation Fairy
Holly the Christmas Fairy
Kylie the Carnival Fairy
Stella the Star Fairy
Shannon the Ocean Fairy
Trixie the Halloween Fairy
Gabriella the Snow Kingdom Fairy
Juliet the Valentine Fairy
Mia the Bridesmaid Fairy
Flora the Dress-Up Fairy
Paige the Christmas Play Fairy
Emma the Easter Fairy
Cara the Camp Fairy
Destiny the Rock Star Fairy
Belle the Birthday Fairy
Olympia the Games Fairy
Selena the Sleepover Fairy
Cheryl the Christmas Tree Fairy
Florence the Friendship Fairy
Lindsay the Luck Fairy

■ SCHOLASTIC

scholastic.com
rainbowmagiconline.com

HIT entertainment

RMSPECIAL10